D0351363

On a Tall Tall Cliff

Aberdeenshire

2144150

To Theo and Ruby
A. S.

First published in hardback in Great Britain by HarperCollins Children's Books in 2004
First published in paperback in 2005

1 3 5 7 9 10 8 6 4 2
ISBN-13: 978-0-00-780971-4

HarperCollins Children's Books is a division of HarperCollins Publishers Ltd.

Text copyright © Andrew Murray 2004
Illustrations copyright © Alan Snow 2004

The author and illustrator assert the moral right to be identified
as the author and illustrator of the work.
A CIP catalogue record for this title is available from the British Library.
All rights reserved. No part of this publication may be reproduced, stored in a retrieval
system or transmitted in any form or by any means, electronic, mechanical, photocopying,
recording or otherwise, without the prior permission of HarperCollins Publishers Ltd,
77-85 Fulham Palace Road, Hammersmith, London W6 8JB.

Visit our website at: www.harpercollinschildrensbooks.co.uk

Printed and bound in Malaysia

On a Tall Tall Tall Cliff

by **Andrew Murray**

illustrated by

Alan Snow

HarperCollins *Children's Books*

On a tall, tall cliff there were two little houses.

The house nearest the edge
was where Puffle lived.
From the edge he could look…

down…

down…

down…

down…

…to the deep, dark
rocks far below.

In the other little house lived Busby.
Busby and Puffle were the very best of friends.

"I'd do anything for you, Busby,"
said Puffle.

"And I'd do anything for you, Puffle,"
said Busby.

One day Busby was busy with lots of papers.
"What are all those for?" asked Puffle.
"Nothing," said Busby. "But while you're here, can I ask you a favour? I need to borrow some things from your garden. Your rake…"

"Of course, I'll go and fetch it," said Puffle.
"And your spade, your watering can and all your flowers and plants," said Busby. "Oh, and your shed, if you can carry it.

It's a lot to ask.
But it will help!"

"That *is* a lot to ask!" thought Puffle, as he walked home. But he went into his garden and collected...

his rake...

his spade...

his watering can...

all his flowers and plants...

…and his garden shed. He could barely lift it.
Huffing and puffing, Puffle
carried everything
to Busby's
house.

"Thank you, Puffle," said Busby, "but I need to borrow some things from your house, too.
Your chair
and your table,
your bath,
and your sofa.
Oh, and your bed, if it's not too heavy.

It's a lot to ask.
But it will really help!"

"That certainly *is* a lot to ask!" thought Puffle, as he walked home. But he went to his house and collected…

…his chair
and his table,
his bath,
his sofa,
and his bed.
It was very heavy!
Sweating and gasping, Puffle carried
everything to Busby's house.

"Thank you so much!" said Busby. "But
I'm afraid I need your roof, too."
"My roof?" cried Puffle.
"Yes, please, and your walls,
and the mice behind them,
your rafters, and the nails in them,
your bricks, and the mortar between them.
And your floorboards,
and the secrets beneath them.
Puffle, I need your whole house.

It's a lot to ask.
But it will really, really help!"

"Busby is making a fool of me," grumbled Puffle, as he trudged home. But he did everything that his friend had asked. He collected…

...his roof, his walls and the mice behind them, his rafters and the nails in them, his bricks and the mortar between them, his floorboards and the secrets beneath them.

Then, huffing and puffing,
sweating and straining,
groaning and grumbling,
he carried his *whole house* to Busby.
"Busby!" gasped Puffle. "This must be enough!
I've brought you my whole house now.'

"LISTEN!" said Busby.
There was a rumbling sound.
It was faint at first, but it grew louder…

and louder…

and louder…

"LOOK!" cried Busby.
A cloud of dust rose up as the
edge of the cliff fell...

down...

down...

down...

down...

...to the deep, dark rocks far below.

CRASH!

"Puffle," smiled Busby, "I have been studying our cliff. All these papers and charts told me that the ground where your house stood would crumble and fall.

My dear friend, you've really, really helped me to help you!"

Puffle thought… then he laughed.
"That's true!" he said. "That's very true!"
Puffle rebuilt his little house next to Busby's, and they lived, the very best of friends, for many long years…

…on that tall, tall cliff,
where you can look from the edge…

down…

down…

down…

down…

…to the deep, dark rocks,
which used to be a cliff,
far below.